Best Day Ever

PAULA EMMENS

Illustrated by Rae Beckett
Edited by Joanne Howton

A GUIDE FOR THE READER

This book has been written for children who might need a self-esteem boost or struggle to get organised when learning new things.

The texts in BLUE are intended to be delivered in a slow,  dreamy way which might feel strange at first. It might help to know that when a child is listening to a story, they are heavily dependant on the subconscious part of their minds and this is a perfect time to make positive suggestions for them to be able to make positive changes, often without realising how the change was made.

When you see the three dots … this indicates a pause in speech. This allows the subconscious time to process what has been suggested.

I truly hope you and your child enjoy this story.

For Tarini, without you, this story would not exist.

A METAPHOR DESIGNED TO BE READ TO CHILDREN AGED 5-9 TO INCREASE SELF-BELIEF AND ORGANISATIONAL SKILLS.

"When we learn new things... you can relax ... and many ideas will come to you. You will take small steps... take your time and then you will see that it is necessary for us to keep practicing and... understand it better now..."

Chapter 1

Friends

The Sun rose slowly and made its way gently up to brighten the morning sky. Chico, the small brown mouse stretched his paws and rubbed his eyes. After a little yawn, he poked his nose out of his burrow to see if anyone else was awake.

It was unusual for Chico to be up at this time. Mice usually sleep until sunset and come out to play at night. Today was different. Chico had heard wonderful things about daytime. His friend Chip had told him stories about the many beautiful colours in the World and of the creatures that played in the meadow by the light of day. Chico had decided that he wanted to see these things for himself.

As he sniffed the morning air and gave his whiskers a wiggle, he started to feel a little uncomfortable and unsure of what might happen today. He was the type of mouse who enjoyed routine. He was comforted by familiarity and knowing what to expect. It felt quite odd to think he would be outside in the daytime, yet he was extremely excited at the same time. He was curious to learn about all the things that usually happen whilst he is curled up in his bed.

As his whiskers twitched in the gentle breeze, a little voice in his head started to tell him that his plan was a bad idea. "What if a cat sees me and chases me?... or a Fox?... Will I be able to run away fast enough?" His tiny heart started to beat a little faster as he began to worry about anything and everything that might possibly go wrong.

A tear rolled down his cheek and he decided he was staying at home. He was just about to snuggle back in his bed when Chip arrived.

"Good morning Chico, are you ready for a fun adventure?" It was not too long before Chip noticed that Chico was looking worried. "Oh, Chico," he spoke in a soft voice, "Is everything okay?"

Chip was a grey squirrel. He had the most magnificent bushy tail. He was exceedingly kind and a good friend to Chico. Every night before he went to bed, he would visit Chico for a nibble of cheese and a chat.  He would tell stories of his daytime adventures and had been encouraging Chico to join him one day so that he could see it with his own eyes.

Chico sniffed and took a deep breath. "Hello Chip, I'm fine but I have decided to stay home today after all because I am worried that I might get chased by a cat and end up being a cat snack"

"Oh Chico, what if you don't end up being chased? What if you miss out on this chance to learn about some magical new things? Just imagine,

you will be able to tell the other mice tonight how brave you are and about all the amazing things that happen in the daytime."

You will be so proud of yourself for just taking your time and giving it a go... one... step... at a time... haven't you?

He stopped for breath. "Anyway, I will look after you. I can't imagine any cat coming near me and if they do, I will just show them my teeth!"

"I really do want to see all the wonderful things, honestly I do but..."

"Great, then what are we waiting for?" Chip interrupted before Chico had the chance to talk his way out of it.

"LET'S GO!"

Chapter 2
The Meadow

The pair set off across the meadow. Chico could not believe how lush and green the grass looked under the Sunlight. The sky was a cool blue with fluffy white clouds floating slowly like cotton wool. Chip was right, daytime truly is magical.

Chico stopped in the middle of the meadow to get a good look and really 'see' all the beautiful things around them. Chip stood over his shoulder to keep a look-out for danger.

The meadow grasses were long but standing on his back legs and with a little stretch, he could just about see above them.

He saw flowers of vibrant reds and blues, all shades of yellows and orange, and wild daisies which were bigger than his tummy! Insects flew by, going about their day. There were busy bees collecting pollen, crane flies and even dragonflies with wings that shimmered in all the colours of the rainbow as the sunlight shone through.

"WOW, THIS IS THE ... BEST ... DAY ... EVER!"

"You see, I told you that you would love it! Come on, there's something special I want you to see" Chip nudged Chico on the hip and merrily scampered towards the edge of the meadow. Chip pointed to something in the bush.

"Here we are, look at this!"

Chico looked. All he could see was a dried up curled brown leaf. He did not understand what was so special about it. Why would Chip choose to show him this?

"What is it? It looks like a dead leaf?"

"Ah, Chico, things are not always what they seem on the surface. Sometimes we need to look a bit deeper. This is my friend... Jeff"

Was he crazy? Has Chip made friends with a leaf?

"Your friend? Seriously? You have given a name to a leaf?" Chico tried hard not to laugh as he held back a little smirk.

Chapter 3
The Leaf

"This isn't a leaf Chico, take a closer look. Do you see something inside? Jeff is actually a caterpillar, and he has got himself stuck in this so called leaf."

Chip spoke to the leaf... listen to this! "Good morning, Jeff, how are you doing today? I have brought my friend Chico to meet you."

To Chico's surprise, the leaf replied.

"Oh, Chip. Thank goodness you're here. I'm feeling sooo stuck today. I feel even bigger than I did yesterday, and it was already pretty cramped in here," Jeff sounded gloomy. "I just don't know what to do, I feel so tired and trapped, I just want things to go back to how they used to be, oh why, oh why, did I build this silly cocoon?"

Chico didn't know what to say but felt he ought to say something. "Hello Jeff, I'm Chico. You seem terribly upset, what happened to you? And what on Earth is a cocoon?"

"I built this cocoon because that is what I was told I had to do. The other caterpillars told me to build a cocoon around myself and wait for 'the change', whatever that means... but ever since then, I have been stuck here hanging about, just waiting and waiting and feeling more and more stuck."

Chip turned to Chico.

"Like I said, Jeff is a caterpillar and today is the perfect day for us to visit him... It's time. Time for the change!"

He turned back towards Jeff.

"Now, Jeff, listen to me, you have had time to rest and like you said you have waited for days. Now is the time for you to push your way out of your cocoon and welcome the change"

"Welcome the change? What change?" Jeff asked

"I don't like the sound of that"

"You will see, trust me." Chip reassured him. "Come on now, I want you to push forwards and stretch your way out of your cocoon, then you will see the beautiful change that you have waited so patiently for."

"I can't do it! It's too difficult, I'll never be able to get out of this silly cocoon, there is no point in trying."

 "Yes, you are right, you can't do it now but after you start pushing yourself, you will see how easily you can do it and you will enjoy the feeling of having done it already,...didn't you?"

Jeff felt a sudden urge to push his way out. He took a long deep breath in, stretched out his legs and felt the cocoon slowly cracking open.

"Keep going, practice makes perfect, you're nearly there."

Chico watched on, silently in awe of his friend Chip. He always knew what to say at times of doubt. Just like he had encouraged him to go out today he was now doing the same for Jeff. He was such a great friend, and he was glad to have him looking over his shoulder. Jeff pushed again with all his might and out he popped.

"I DID IT! I DID IT! I ACTUALLY DID IT!" Jeff exclaimed.

Chapter 4
Freedom

Exhausted from his escape to freedom, Jeff clung on to the cocoon with his legs.

"I am so tired now and so happy to be free again, but I feel different. Do I look different to you Chip?"

"Yes Jeff, you look different," Chip smiled. "The change has happened. You waited patiently and you have grown your wings. You will need to unfold them carefully and let them dry in the breeze before you can fly"

Jeff unfurled his wings. They were so bright and beautiful. Jeff smiled a cheesy grin from ear to ear. He was so proud of himself even if he didn't quite understand what had just happened.

He had wings! He wasn't a caterpillar anymore, he was a bright, colourful butterfly. He loved the change.

Chico could not believe what was happening right before his eyes. 'How is it possible for a caterpillar to grow wings and fly? Just wait until I tell the other mice' He thought to himself.

Jeff's wings were stunning. They were bright orange with swirly black patterns. They were perfectly symmetrical just like a mirror image. He couldn't stop looking at his magnificent wings.

"I...I...I.. c...can't believe it! I, I'm a b...beautiful butterfly!" Jeff stuttered with delight.

"Of course, you are. Now, it's time to fly! Off you go, and remember to have fun"

Jeff flapped his wings and up and away he flew. Chico and Chip watched him take his first flight around the meadow.

"What do you think of that then Chico?"

"I think that is awesome!"

The pair tried to keep up with Jeff from the ground and had lots of fun playing together. Every time Jeff flew nearby, they could hear the delighted sounds of Jeff's newfound freedom.

"Wa- hee!" "Whoosh!" "Weeeeee!"

It was getting late and after such an amazing day, Chico was keen to get back home to tell the other mice about his adventures.

As they walked back, Chico thanked Chip for giving him the chance to learn so much.

"Chip, you are the best friend I could ever wish for. I didn't think today would be this much fun. It is because of you that I was brave enough to learn new things. I felt safe and there was nothing to worry about at all. You helped Jeff to be brave too when he didn't think he could break free. Everyone could do with a friend like you"

"You mean to say it is good to have a Chip on your shoulder?" They both laughed.

This was a day Chico would never forget.

Self Esteem

Children who feel good about themselves have more confidence to try new things. When we have a good self-esteem, we are better able to cope with mistakes and this develops resilience. Here are some things you can do with your child to help them to feel good about themselves;

Tips to improving Self-Esteem

1. Learn something new
2. Do kind things for others
3. Make new friends
4. Ask yourself what your best friend/teacher/mum thinks about you
5. Set yourself achievable goals
6. Always talk to yourself using positive language.
7. Rather than "I can't do maths" say "I will practice maths and will get better at it"
8. Practice positive affirmations

About the Author

Paula is a child therapist and coach living in Kent, the garden of England. Her mission is to help young people build bright, happy futures for themselves. Knowing how powerful metaphors can be, she often writes stories to help her clients make positive changes at an unconscious level. Her stories are created using a combination of hypnotic language and word weaving for the subconscious part of our minds to later process and decode the hidden messages.

www.mindyoukent.co.uk